3

One wet Saturday, Oliver was stuck inside.

He stared through the window and wondered

if the rain would ever stop.

"You could play a game inside," said Mum.

"Sitting still is boring," moaned Oliver.

"It's been wet play all week in school.

We didn't get to run at all."

"If it stops raining later we can go out

to the woods for you to run," said Mum.

At last, the sun came out. Mum and Oliver
went to the woods.

"Go slowly. It's a bit muddy," Mum said.

But Oliver wanted to run fast. He was
so happy to be outside.

Oliver jumped over a log and slipped.

"Owwww!" he cried. "My leg hurts!"

Oliver went to the hospital for an X-ray. His leg was broken. It was put into plaster and he had to use crutches and rest.

"My leg really hurts," he moaned, "and I can't run! It's so boring!"

"It's nice to be cosy inside in winter," said Mum. "Why don't you watch sport on TV?"

But watching other people running made Oliver more miserable.

Mum wanted to cheer Oliver up.

She had an idea.

"Why don't we ask Grandad to come and stay?" she said.

Grandad arrived with a suitcase and

a big box.

"What's in there?" Oliver asked.

"Some things to stop you from being bored

while you have to sit still," Grandad said.

He lifted out a chess set. "Do you want

to play chess?"

"Um, OK," said Oliver.

Oliver didn't really feel like playing chess,

but he thought it was better than sitting still

and doing nothing.

Oliver and Grandad sat by the window and

set up the chess board.

11

Grandad looked up from the chess board and saw a bird in the garden outside.

"A robin!" he said. "Does it visit that tree often, Oliver?"

Oliver had no idea. He always ran around the garden and the birds always flew away.

"There are some things you can only see if you sit still," Grandad said.

Grandad reached into his box again.

He picked up a book about birds. Then he took out a pair of binoculars.

"What are those for?" Oliver asked.

He took the binoculars from Grandad and looked through them. Suddenly, the trees looked much bigger and closer.

"Binoculars can help us find out what kinds of birds come to your garden," Grandad said. "You could be a bird spotter."

13

Oliver enjoyed looking for the birds in his garden. It really kept him from getting bored. He and Grandad sat by the window every day.

"I can see a small red bird. What is it, Grandad?" Oliver asked.

"Well spotted, Oliver. Let's look it up in the bird book," Grandad said, turning the pages. "Aha, here it is. It's a crossbill." Grandad opened a notebook. "Let's keep a wildlife diary," he said. "We can write the names of the birds that we see."

Oliver spotted more and more birds to write in his wildlife diary:

Blackbird. Song thrush. Bullfinch. Wagtail.

One morning it looked very cold outside. The grass was covered with frost. The trees looked bare with no leaves on their branches. "Winter can be a hard time for wildlife," Grandad said. "Let's put some food out for the birds. Then more birds might visit."

Oliver sprinkled breadcrumbs on the grass. Grandad helped Oliver make a home-made bird feeder. They covered a pine cone with lard and then rolled it in seeds. They tied some string around it and hung it on a tree. The birds loved it.

After a week, Grandad had to go home.

Oliver was really disappointed.

"Keep on writing in your wildlife diary,"

Grandad said. "I keep a diary at my house too.

Next time I see you we can tell each other what

birds we've spotted."

A few days later, a parcel arrived.

Oliver unwrapped it excitedly. Grandad had sent

a book about birds, just like his. It would help

Oliver find out the names of the birds he saw.

Even better, it suggested what to feed them

and other ways of looking after them.

Dear Oliver,

I hope you enjoy using this book. Have you seen any more bullfinches or song thrushes? Keep looking after them, and I'm sure you'll see plenty more birds in your garden.

Take care,

Grandad

PS How is your leg?

Oliver smiled. Now he could take care of his leg **and** the birds in his garden. He was so glad Grandad had come to stay.

Story order

Look at these 5 pictures and captions.
Put the pictures in the right order
to retell the story.

1

Oliver starts a wildlife diary.

2

Oliver breaks his leg.

3

Oliver says goodbye to Grandad.

4

Grandad spots a robin.

5

Oliver and Grandad feed the birds.

Independent Reading

This series is designed to provide an opportunity for your child to read on their own. These notes are written for you to help your child choose a book and to read it independently.

In school, your child's teacher will often be using reading books that have been banded to support the process of learning to read. Use the book band colour your child is reading in school to help you make a good choice. *Grandad Comes to Stay* is a good choice for children reading at White Band in their classroom to read independently.

The aim of independent reading is to read this book with ease, so that your child enjoys the story and relates it to their own experiences.

About the book

Oliver loves to run. He never sits still or moves slowly ... until an injury forces him to take it easy. Lucky for Oliver, Grandad comes round to help, and he shows Oliver how to have fun during his slow winter.

Before reading

Help your child to learn how to make good choices by asking: "Why did you choose this book? Why do you think you will enjoy it?" Ask your child about what they know about bird spotting. Then look at the cover with your child and ask: "Do you know anyone who likes to spot birds? How do you think it makes a bird spotter feel when they see a new type of bird?"

Remind your child that they can break words into groups of syllables or sound out letters to make a word if they get stuck.

Decide together whether your child will read the story independently or read it aloud to you.

During reading

Remind your child of what they know and what they can do independently. If reading aloud, support your child if they hesitate or ask for help by telling the word. If reading to themselves, remind your child that they can come and ask for your help if stuck.

After reading

Support comprehension by asking your child to tell you about the story. Use the story order puzzle to encourage your child to retell the story in the right sequence, in their own words. The correct sequence can be found on the next page.

Help your child think about the messages in the book that go beyond the story and ask: "What do you think Oliver learned about his likes and dislikes when he was forced to slow down?"

Give your child a chance to respond to the story: "What was your favourite part of the story? Would you like to keep a wildlife diary?"

Extending learning

Help your child predict other possible outcomes of the story by asking: "What if Grandad hadn't spotted a bird while they played chess? What other new skills might Oliver have learned from his grandad?"

In the classroom, your child's teacher may be teaching different kinds of sentences. The story contains several examples you can look at together, including statements, commands, exclamations and questions. Find these together and point out how the end punctuation can help us understand the meaning of the sentence.

Franklin Watts
First published in Great Britain in 2020
by The Watts Publishing Group

Series Editors: Jackie Hamley and Melanie Palmer and Grace Glendinning
Series Advisors: Dr Sue Bodman and Glen Franklin
Series Designers: Peter Scoulding and Cathryn Gilbert

A CIP catalogue record for this book is
available from the British Library.

ISBN 978 1 4451 7226 2 (hbk)
ISBN 978 1 4451 7227 9 (pbk)
ISBN 978 1 4451 7231 6 (library ebook)
ISBN 978 1 4451 7929 2 (ebook)

Printed in China

Franklin Watts
An imprint of
Hachette Children's Group
Part of The Watts Publishing Group
Carmelite House
50 Victoria Embankment
London EC4Y 0DZ

An Hachette UK Company
www.hachette.co.uk

www.reading-champion.co.uk

Answer to Story order: 2, 4, 1, 5, 3